The Princess and the Shoe

For Andrew,
who believes in me, even when
I forget to believe in myself –
C. H.

For Denise who started running
and just ran and ran . . .
S. W.

First published in 2019 by Nosy Crow Ltd
14 Baden Place, Crosby Row, London SE1 1YW
www.nosycrow.com

978 1 78800 335 3 (HB)
978 1 78800 336 0 (PB)

Nosy Crow and associated logos are trademarks
and/or registered trademarks of Nosy Crow Ltd.

Text copyright © Caryl Hart 2019
Illustrations copyright © Sarah Warburton 2019

The right of Caryl Hart to be identified as the author and Sarah Warburton
to be identified as the illustrator of this work has been asserted.

A CIP catalogue record for this book is available from the British Library.

Printed in China
Papers used by Nosy Crow are made from
wood grown in sustainable forests.

1 3 5 7 9 8 6 4 2 (HB)
1 3 5 7 9 8 6 4 2 (PB)

The Princess and the Shoe

Caryl Hart

Sarah Warburton

PALACE

TOWN

WOODS

nosy crow

A princess called Jasmine lived far, far away
With two lovely stepsisters, Gracie and Faye.
But unlike SOME girls who love ribbons and bows,
She hated long dresses and other smart clothes.

Once, Jasmine was stuck having no fun at all,
As she tried a new gown for her Big Birthday Ball.

The tailor cried, "Jasmine, please try to stand still!
Don't wriggle and fidget –
You're making me ill!"

Her sisters called, "Jasmine, come practise your twirls.
Go slowly – be graceful like all royal girls."
But Jasmine thought whizzing round fast was more fun.

"Stop NOW!" Gracie gasped.
"A princess must not run!

You won't meet your prince if you rush round like that.
Princesses stand still, smile and wear a nice hat!"
"Your ball is quite soon," Faye said, "this is your chance!
A nice prince might kiss you – or ask you to dance!"

"What – ME? Kiss a BOY?" Jasmine spluttered. "No way!
It's true, I might want to get married one day.
But now's not the time. I've got too much to do.
You think they're so great? Get a prince to kiss YOU!"

Next day, at parade, Jasmine said to the queen.
"Those children are running about on the green!
They seem so alive in the wind and the sun.
Oh, please may I join them? It looks like such fun."

"Gosh, no!" gasped the queen. "You'd get muddy and wet!
Princesses can't run, don't be silly, my pet.
You're meant to look pretty, smile sweetly, be calm.
No prince wants a sweaty princess on his arm!"

But back in her library, reading a book,
Young Jasmine heard laughter from down by the brook.
A group of small children were running a race,
She watched as they played, a big grin on her face.

"Hello!" Jasmine called.
"Please, could I join in too?"

The children just laughed.
"What, a princess like you?
Princesses can't run.
You might lose your gold crown.
Your dress might get dirty!
Your socks might fall down!"

"Oh dear!" Jasmine sighed.
"Why is life so unfair?
I just want to run with the wind in my hair.

But look! What's this poster, taped onto the wall?
NEXT SUNDAY!
Cross Country Race!
Open to All!

Oh, gosh!" Jasmine gasped. "Is this true? Let me see . . .
It really says 'all' so that MUST include me!
I'll enter the race and amaze everyone.
I'll prove to this town that a princess can run!"

The very next day, Jasmine jumped out of bed.
"If I want to race, I must practise," she said.

But when she got lost
in a dark scary wood,

She cried, "Oh dear me.
It's too hard. I'm no good."
But she didn't give up
and soon came to a pond.

She raced through the grounds,

past the town and beyond.

Her confidence grew . . .
until tragedy struck –
She met with some sheep
and got thoroughly stuck!

PALACE

TOWN

WOODS

"Oh heck!" Jasmine thought, and she wanted to cry,
But told herself, "No. You will have one more try."

It would have gone well but she tripped on a log
And fell with a squelch in a great gloopy bog.
Her shouts reached a prince, who was out for a ride.
"A maid in distress! I shall save her!" he cried.

But when he saw Jasmine, he grimaced, "Oh, YUCK!
I can't rescue you! You're all covered in muck!"

When Jasmine got home, the queen sighed, "What a mess!
Your knees are all muddy and look at your dress!
Your ball is this Sunday! Come now, wash your face . . ."
"Oh, no!" Jasmine thought. "That's the day of my race!

The ball might be fun, but I want to race too!
A super-fast runner could do both, it's true.
But there is no way I could run fast enough.
I WISH things were different. My life is so tough!"

Poor Jasmine was gloomy and moody that night.
"My dream is just silly. The others were right.
If dainty and pretty are what I should be,
Could finding a prince be the best thing for me?"

Just then, with a SWOOSH and a magical spark,
A fairy appeared, right outside in the dark.
"It's nearly your birthday. I'll grant you your wish."
And she wiggled her magic wand –
SWISHETY-SWISH!

"A new pair of shoes! Golly gosh," Jasmine cried.
"With springy white soles and red stripes down the side!"
"They'll make you run fast," said the fairy. "But hey,
The magic runs out when the clock strikes midday."

The day of the ball,
Jasmine pulled on her crown,
Then crept through the door
and ran off towards town.

"Here goes," Jasmine thought,
as she stood at the start,
New shoes on her feet
and a thrill in her heart.

The clock chimed eleven. They started the race!
Young Jasmine set off at a very fast pace.
At this rate, she'd finish in no time at all
And have lots of time to get back for the ball!

She sped over fields and dashed round the big wood.

"My legs feel so strong," Jasmine gasped, "I feel good!"

She squelched through some mud then she let out a scream.

"My SHOE!" Jasmine cried. "It's been washed down the stream!"

As the runners sped past, harsh thoughts swirled round her head.

"Princesses should try to be pretty," they said.

"Princesses should think buying dresses is fun.

Don't try to be different. Princesses CAN'T run!"

A feeling welled up from a place deep inside . . .

. . . And burst from her mouth, "Yes, I CAN!" Jasmine cried.

"I'll finish this race wearing only ONE shoe!
I'll prove to them all what this princess CAN DO!"

The crowd cheered and clapped.
Jasmine picked up the pace . . .

. . . And flew to the finish! She'd WON her first race!

"Bravo!" cheered the fairy. "I knew you could win!"
"It's thanks to your shoes," Jasmine said with a grin.
"They weren't really magic," the kind fairy smiled,
"You won because you were determined, my child!"

"The magic you used came from inside your head.
You had to BELIEVE you could do it," she said.
"Your dreams are important, they're what make you, YOU.
Let nobody tell you there's things you can't do."

Then Jasmine's whole family pushed through the crowd.

"My darling!" the queen said. "You've made us so proud!"

"What, really?" cried Jasmine. "You're not cross or mad?"

"You've proved us all wrong," smiled the king, "and we're glad."

The prince sidled up with a crown on his head.

"Whoever this shoe fits, I'll marry!" he said.

"Hooray!" Jasmine cheered. "You have rescued my shoe . . .

But, sorry, there's no way I'm marrying YOU!"

They partied that night at the Big Birthday Ball,
With fancy food, cake, games, and prizes for all.

And now, just like Jasmine, we know that it's true . . .

. . . There's no end to the things that a princess
CAN DO!